Angelfish
Feels Angry

Franklin Watts
First published in Great Britain in 2021 by Hodder & Stoughton

Credits
Series Editor: Sarah Peutrill
Series Designer: Sarah Peden

ISBN: 978 1 4451 7403 7 (hardback)
ISBN: 978 1 4451 7404 4 (paperback)

Printed in China

Franklin Watts
An imprint of
Hachette Children's Group
Part of Hodder & Stoughton
Carmelite House
50 Victoria Embankment
London EC4Y 0DZ

An Hachette UK Company
www.hachette.co.uk

www.hachettechildrens.co.uk

THE Emotion OCEAN

Angelfish Feels Angry

by Katie Woolley and David Arumi

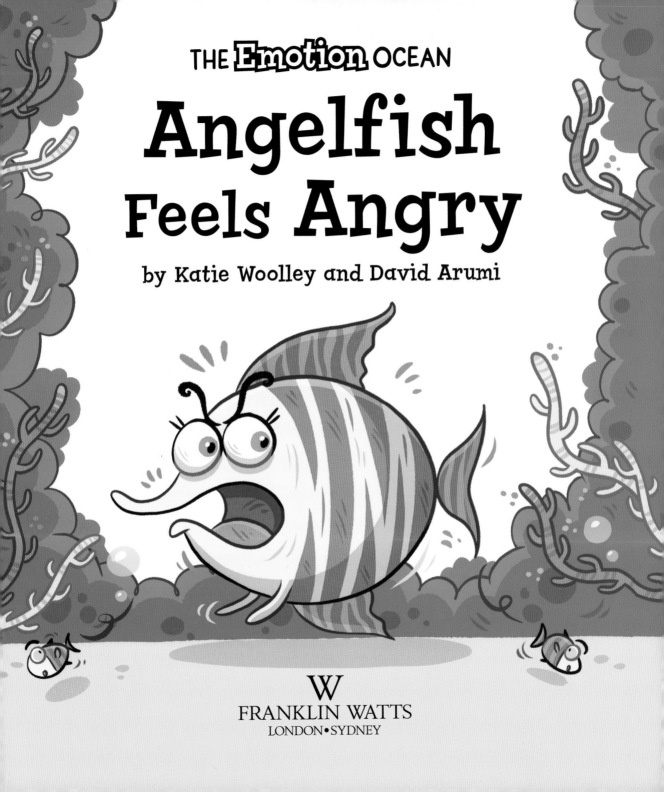

W
FRANKLIN WATTS
LONDON•SYDNEY

It was a busy day at Sea School.

Shark was reading a book.

Starfish and Swordfish were in the role-play area dressed as dinosaurs!

Whale was practising her maths and Angelfish was painting a picture.

Jellyfish was playing in the sand pit.

Angelfish swam backwards to look at her picture. She fell over Whale's big tail fin and bumped into the table.

Up, up, up went her paint pots.
Down, down, down they fell with a
SPLAT!

"Oops, sorry!" said Whale.

Angelfish felt her face go red. She started
to shake.

"You've ruined my picture!" she shouted at her friend.

Angelfish shouted so loudly that Whale whooshed away and hid in the book corner.

Then Angelfish threw her picture on the floor and swam off in a stream of angry bubbles.

Shark found Angelfish in the home corner.
There was a deep frown on her red face.

Shark felt very sad. Sometimes, Angelfish could be very angry indeed.

Mr Narwhal found Angelfish crying.

"Whale ruined my picture!" she cried.

"It was an accident," said Mr Narwhal gently. "And you did get very angry …"

Angelfish thought for a moment. Soon, she felt sorry.

"I was so angry with Whale that I was unkind," she sniffed.

"Do you know what I do when I feel angry?" asked Mr Narwhal.

"You get angry, too?" gasped Angelfish.

Mr Narwhal smiled. "Of course! We all feel angry sometimes."

"What do you do when you feel angry?" asked Angelfish.

"I breathe in and count to three. Then think of what makes me happy. Why don't you give it a try?"

Angelfish breathed in 1, 2, 3.

"My friends make me happy," she smiled.

"Then go and tell them you're sorry!" said Mr Narwhal. "And next time you feel angry, breathe in and count to three. Then think of what makes you happy."

Angelfish swam back to her friends. They were playing hide and seek in the playground.

Angelfish spotted Whale's big tail this time!
It was next to Shark's big fin.

"I'm sorry I got cross with you," she said to her friends.

"You were very loud, Angelfish," Whale whispered.

"Thank you for saying sorry," said Shark.

Just then, the bell rang for the end of playtime.
The animals swam back to class.

Whale and Shark looked at Angelfish's painting.

"I've got an idea," Whale said.

The three friends painted a new picture.

"It's a picture of what makes me happy!"
said Angelfish.

Emotions are BIG!

Your feelings are a big part of you, just like they are a big part of Angelfish and her friends. Look at the pictures and talk about these feelings. Here are some questions to help you:

How did Angelfish feel when her painting was knocked over?

What happened to her face and body when she felt cross?

How did her friends feel
when Angelfish shouted
at them?

What activity helped
Angelfish stop
feeling angry?

How did Angelfish and
her friends feel at the
end of the story?

What could YOU do to
calm down when you
feel angry?

31

Let's Talk About Feelings

The Emotion Ocean series has been written to help young children begin to understand their own feelings, and how those feelings and subsequent actions affect themselves and others.

It provides a starting point for parents, carers and teachers to discuss BIG feelings with little learners. The series is set in the ocean with a class of animal friends who experience these big emotions in familiar, everyday scenarios.

Angelfish Feels Angry

This story looks at the emotion of anger, how it makes you feel, how you react to the feeling of being angry and how your actions have an impact on others around you.

The book aims to encourage children to identify their own feelings, consider how they can affect their own happiness and the happiness of others, and offer simple tools to help manage their emotions.

How to use the book

The book is designed for adults to share with either an individual child, or a group of children, and as a starting point for discussion.

Choose a time when you and the children are relaxed and have time to share the story.

Before reading the story:

• Spend time looking at the illustrations and talking about what the book might be about before reading it together.

• Encourage children to employ a 'phonics-first' approach to tackling new words by sounding them out.

After reading the story:

• Talk about the story with the children. Ask them to describe Angelfish's feelings. Ask them if how she behaved at the start was a good idea. Why or why not?

• Ask the children why they think it is important to understand their feelings. Does it make them feel better to understand why they feel the way they do in certain situations? Does it help them get along with others?

• Place the children into groups. Ask them to think of a time they have felt cross. How did they react? What did they do to stop feeling angry?

• At the end of the session, invite a spokesperson from each group to read out their list to the others. Then discuss the different lists as a whole class.